Customer Service: 1-877-277-9441 or customerservice@pikidsmedia.com

Published by Phoenix International Publications, Inc.

8501 West Higgins Road   59 Gloucester Place
Chicago, Illinois 60631   London W1U 8JJ

www.pikidsmedia.com

PI Kids and *we make books come alive* are trademarks of
Phoenix International Publications, Inc., and are registered
in the United States.

Look and Find is a trademark of Phoenix International Publications, Inc.,
and is registered in the United States and Canada.

8 7 6 5 4 3 2 1

ISBN: 978-1-5037-4359-5

Disney
FROZEN

Adapted by Jennifer H. Keast and Emily Skwish
Illustrated by Art Mawhinney

we make books come alive®
Phoenix International Publications, Inc.
Chicago • London • New York • Hamburg • Mexico City • Sydney

Meet the Characters

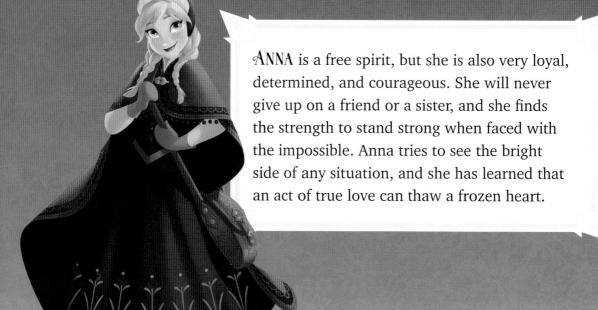

ANNA is a free spirit, but she is also very loyal, determined, and courageous. She will never give up on a friend or a sister, and she finds the strength to stand strong when faced with the impossible. Anna tries to see the bright side of any situation, and she has learned that an act of true love can thaw a frozen heart.

ELSA works hard to be a good ruler, sister, and friend. Although she can be quiet and reserved, she is fierce and larger than life when she sets her snowy powers free! With a heart that is bigger than she knows, Elsa has learned that love can conquer fear. Will she soon learn the reason she was born with her powers?

OLAF is a snowman who loves warm hugs! Elsa created him using her magic, and he has been a true friend ever since. Curious, full of wonder, and funny as a snowman who loves summer, Olaf wants to help and be friends with everyone. After all, there are some folks in life who are worth melting for.

KRISTOFF was raised by trolls, his best friend is a reindeer, and he works as a solitary ice harvester. He doesn't know many humans— or much about them—but once he met Anna, things changed. Now, when he's not working hard at harvesting ice or strumming his lute with Sven, Kristoff is thinking about starting a big family with Anna.

SVEN doesn't speak to his best friend Kristoff using *words*, but this heroic and resourceful reindeer is able to communicate so much. A simple snort or tilt of his antlers lets Kristoff know his opinion on the matter at hand. Whether it's saving Anna or saving Arendelle, Sven is there to help Kristoff do his best. And to eat carrots.

When Princess Anna first discovers her sister Elsa's magical power, she thinks it's wonderful!

Look around to find these icy things the two sisters made.

this igloo   snow angel   this flurry of snow   this sledding hill   pyramid of snowballs   Olaf the snowman

After Elsa accidentally puts a white streak in Anna's hair, the king worries she may hurt her little sister. Elsa decides to stay away from Anna to keep her safe.

Look around for these things that Anna would like to share with her sister:

 ice cream cones

 dollhouse

 jump rope

 chess game

 wishbone

 these dolls

Once the townspeople see Elsa's icy magic, they become frightened. To avoid hurting someone with her powers, Elsa runs away.

As she flees, look around the courtyard for these frozen creations:

this flag   icy lantern   this fountain   this topiary   this topiary   this stone

Anna climbs up the mountain to find Elsa, but soon realizes she needs help.
A mountain man named Kristoff seems to have the know-how.

Kristoff agrees to help Anna, but soon wonders whether that was a good idea!

While they flee the wolves, look for Kristoff's scattered belongings:

 scorched blanket

 broken lute

 sweater

 sock

 hat

mitten

Anna finds her sister and asks Elsa to come home. But it will take some convincing to get Elsa to agree.

As Elsa creates a snowman named Marshmallow, look for these other icy items she has made:

Summer has finally returned to Arendelle! To thank Kristoff for helping her, Anna gives him a brand-new sled and some carrots for Sven.

Return to the two young sisters playing in the snow to find these items that could decorate a snowman:

carrot for nose

this lump of coal

branch for arm

these mittens

big button

this winter hat

Skip back to the scenes of the sisters growing up and search for these things that Anna enjoys solo:

knitting needles

yo-yo

guitar

book

tricycle

swing

Arendelle's visitors did not travel light! Go back to the docks to find these supplies:

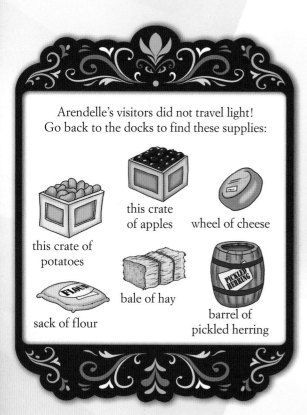

this crate of apples

wheel of cheese

this crate of potatoes

bale of hay

sack of flour

barrel of pickled herring

As Elsa flees Arendelle, look for these frightened townspeople:

Go back to Oaken's Trading Post to find these troll souvenirs that are for sale:

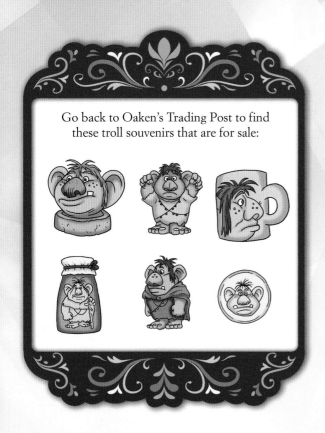

Run back to the wolves and identify these animal tracks in the snow:

bear

moose

arctic fox

musk ox

beaver

horse

Return to Elsa's dazzling ice palace to find these unique ice creations:

Search the streets of Arendelle to find these six pairs of sisters enjoying the summer sun:

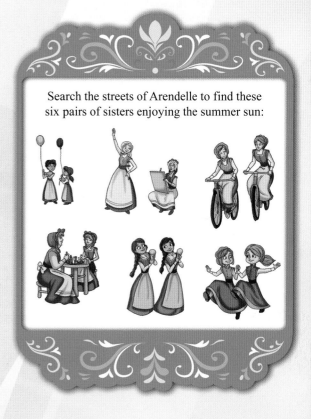

King Agnarr tells the best bedtime stories—especially if you like intense tales with lots of fighting. Fortunately, young Anna and Elsa like all kinds of stories. This one happens to be about the day their father became King of Arendelle during a clash with the Northuldra. "The past has a way of returning," the king warns. Nighty-night!

While the sisters fall asleep, look around the cozy bedroom for some reminders of the past:

Arendellian shield

this wall hanging

this book

this painting

this portrait of King Runeard

Queen Iduna's scarf

Many years later, Elsa is Queen of Arendelle. She begins hearing a voice, one that only she can hear. It calls her out of the castle, and it speaks to a part of her that no one has ever connected with before. As she listens, she reaches out to the voice with her magic. To Elsa's surprise, beautiful figures made of snow and ice form all around her. They could be the keys to Arendelle's past—and future.

Spot these crystalline creations:

ice wind-swirl

ice giant

ice salamander

ice water-horse

this ice tree

this ice tree

Elsa, Anna, Kristoff, Olaf, and Sven approach a mist-covered forest and discover four large monoliths, each with an ancient symbol representing one of the four elements: Earth, Fire, Water, and Wind. No one knows what secrets and adventures await in this enchanted place.

Search the scene for these mist-ical things:

this flower   this flower   this plant   this plant   fire symbol   wind symbol

In the forest, the friends are introduced to the spirits of nature. The Wind Spirit makes an entrance that blows them away. Now they are stuck in a swirling vortex that has them spinning, twisting, and feeling more than a little sick.

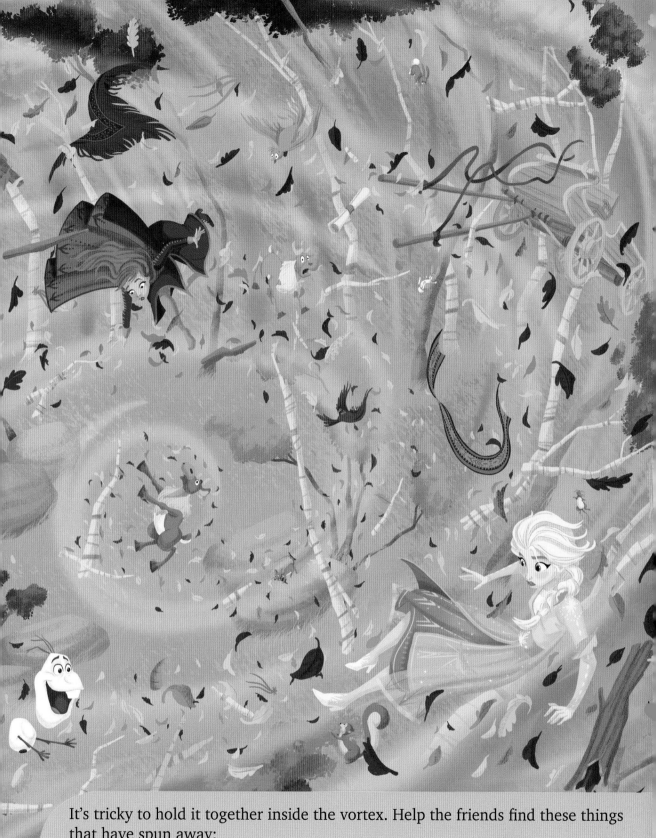

It's tricky to hold it together inside the vortex. Help the friends find these things that have spun away:

Kristoff's ring

Anna's boot

Kristoff's belt

Sven's harness

Queen Iduna's scarf

Olaf's nose

On the journey, Elsa and her friends meet the Northuldra, an ancient, nomadic people. They also meet several Arendellian soldiers who have been trapped along with the Northuldra in the Enchanted Forest for thirty-four years. Suddenly, the Fire Spirit arrives on the scene. This excitable amphibian is a real trail blazer. As it scurries, it leaves a fiery path that threatens to send the forest up in flames!

Can you keep your cool as you find these people of Northuldra and Arendelle?

Yelena

Honeymaren

Ryder

Mattias

this Northuldra soldier

this Northuldra soldier

As the friends learn more about the history of the Northuldra, they are discovered by Earth Giants. These behemoths sense Elsa's magic in the air, and they come sniff-sniff-sniffing to find her. Elsa quickly steps in to create a diversion that sends the Earth Giants on their lumbering way.

It's a giant task, but you can do it! Find these tiny things:

this red squirrel · this shrew · this lemming · this otter · this arctic fox · this hedgehog

Elsa knows that the journey to discover the secrets of her power will be dangerous. She creates an ice boat for Anna and Olaf and sends them away from her, to safety. The only problem is, Anna accidentally steers them past a riverbank where the Earth Giants are taking their afternoon nap.

As Anna and Olaf row their boat gently—very, very gently—down the stream, locate these dreaming Giants:

Elsa sets out on her own to find the secret of her power, and she encounters another force of nature, the Water Spirit. Is it a fish? A whale? No, the Water Nokk is a majestic horse that embodies the power of water. Elsa must earn its respect before it will let her reach her destination.

Dive in and find these icy blasts:

Tiptoe back to the bedtime story and search for these items that foreshadow the future:

this book

this drawing of Olaf

ship in a bottle

Elsa's gloves

this toy reindeer

this painting

Skate back to Elsa's icy creations and collect these shimmering crystals before they melt:

Journey back to the monoliths and find this fantastical foliage:

Blow back to the Wind Spirit and catch these spiraling things:

this tree

this bird

sleigh

this reindeer

this log

Anna's book

Blaze a trail back to the Fire Spirit and find these things that will *not* go up in smoke today:

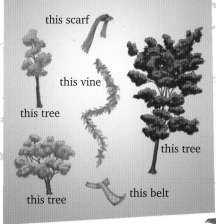

this scarf

this vine

this tree

this tree

this tree

this belt

Thunder back to the Earth Giants and find these other examples of magic at work:

Wind Spirit

this snowflake

this ice crystal

this snowflake

Fire Spirit

this snowflake

There's something fishy about the river. Slip back to the ice boat and find these splishy and splashy things:

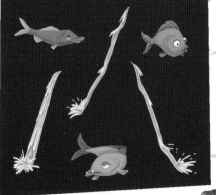

Swim (or gallop) back to the Water Spirit and identify these rugged rock formations: